... and in the African-American tradition of animal folktales, as found in *The People Could Fly*, the animals in *Jaguarundi* can talk.

The story parallels humans who escape their homelands in search of better, safer lives. I was astounded to discover the added bonus, with the animals, of a classic symbolism of fleeing North — crossing the Great River into a Promised Land. I didn't plan it; nothing was further from my mind. But the symbolism was indeed organic and was to me a wonderful revelation about this book.

*— excerpt from a speech by Virginia Hamilton at*
*the Tenth Annual Virginia Hamilton Conference*
*in Kent, Ohio, on April 15, 1994*

# JAGUARUNDI

## Virginia Hamilton

WITH PAINTINGS BY
## Floyd Cooper

SCHOLASTIC INC.

New York   Toronto   London   Auckland   Sydney

In memory of Earth's animals no longer here,
and in praise of those that still survive
— V. H.

For the bearers of the torches that lead us home
— F. C.

ISBN 0-590-47367-0

Text copyright © 1995 by Virginia Hamilton
Illustrations copyright © 1995 by Floyd Cooper
All rights reserved. Published by Scholastic Inc.

Blue Ribbon Signature is a trademark of Scholastic Inc.

12 11 10 9 8 7 6 5 4 3 2 1      2      7 8 9/9 0 1 2/0

Printed in the United States of America          08

RUNDI JAGUARUNDI stalks in the sunset shadows. His coat is the blue-gray shade of scrubland at twilight. Once, this was the rain forest wild, but years ago, settlers began clearing the timber. They built houses and barns, and fences. Pineapple ranchers and longhorn cattle herders came to stay.

Rundi stays out of sight. Always on the move, he prowls, keeps watch. He murmurs, "The forest canopy is going. I'm afraid we wild animals will go with it."

In the morning, he creeps along the lowland edge. He comes upon Coati Coatimundi, who is nosing and sniffing in the plowed field hedges. "You old Coati," he growls, softly, "what in the hot breezes are you up to today?"

Coati crawls out from beneath a scrub. His bushy tail stands straight up, like a walking stick with a curved tip. "Old friend!" Coati says. His great nose wiggles. He tiptoes and sways, almost dancing over to Rundi.

They go off to a shady spot among the spiny bromeliads. "I'm going to be moving on," Rundi says. "But to leave friends always makes me sad. Coati, would you like to come along?"

"Come along—where to? To do what?" asks Coati.

"To find a better place to live," answers Rundi. "Where high, leafy branches still make a crown canopy."

"Don't mind if I do!" says Coati. "Which way do we go?"

"I've heard that to the north lies a great river called Rio Bravo," Rundi says. "They say there is timberland and a few small farms. There are animals like you and me, Coati. We could settle down for good."

Off they go, Rundi and Coati. They greet Kit Fox, wandering. Fox yips a swift hello.

"You're a long way from home," says Rundi.

"I was captured for my coat and carried south. But I got away," says Fox.

"There's danger here, too," says Rundi. "So we're going north to the Rio Bravo waters. Come north with us, Fox. We hope to find a canopy."

"I'll think about it," Fox says.

"Tell everyone where to find us," says Rundi. "Before we leave, we'll meet at midnight at the Great Pineapple Field of the Fallen Timber. Everyone knows where that is."

"I know the field," says Fox. "Whoever I see I will tell."

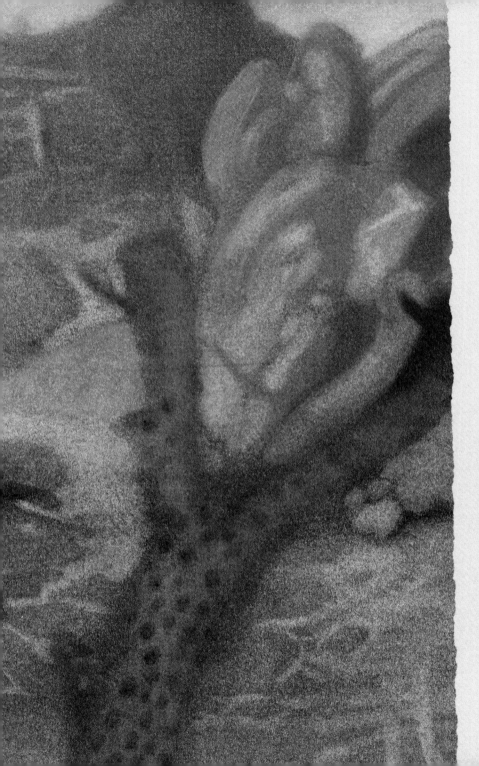

Running on, Fox spies Owl Monkey, who sleeps by day. "Wake up!" he yips. "Rundi and Coati plan to go north to the Rio Bravo waters. Tonight they'll be in the Great Pineapple Field of the Fallen Timber. Come say good-bye. Tell everybody."

"I will," hoots the monkey. He makes a funnel of his lips and barks, "ANIMALS, SAY GOOD-BYE TONIGHT TO OUR FRIENDS, JAGUARUNDI AND COATIMUNDI. THEY'RE LEAVING THIS PLACE...." He passes along the whole message.

Bush Dog hears Owl Monkey's news. So does shy
Spotted Cavy. Bush Dog shouts at Maned Wolf, streaking
by, "Stop, brother Wolf, so far from your home. Stop!"
Wolf stops, and Bush Dog tells him the news.
    Maned Wolf is a fine, wild beast, with tall, black legs
like stilts. "I'll come," he tells Bush Dog. He races off at
high speed. Far and wide, east and west, he tells the news.

So many animal friends hear about Rundi and Coati leaving. That night, they all make their way to the Great Pineapple Field of the Fallen Timber. Howler Monkey comes alone, whistling softly. He is followed by Kit Fox. Fox's plume-shaped tail trembles in the air. White-throated Capuchin Monkey is there. All three are rarely seen in the open.

Capuchin leaps upon a fallen timber log, as does Howler. The log is broken and split. They scramble back and forth, from log-piece to chunk, looking for places to hide. Soon, they vanish in the deep dark of the vast Great Pineapple Field.

Ringtail Cat finds its way, and so does White-tailed Deer. Tayra, Kinkajou, and Bobcat are among the last. All move around, talking low. They find their places.

Rundi leaps upon a split piece of log. His glowing eyes and glistening coat gleam in the full-moon night.

His friends crouch and stretch. Their coats ripple. They lay low. They are dark shapes, shielded by the swordlike pineapple leaves. The moon above is a cottony light, spread like a long, thin mesh over the vast field, and them.

"So glad you've come," begins Rundi. Shy Coati Coatimundi reveals himself behind pineapples. He jumps gingerly on a broken chunk of log. Coati's bushy tail sways, lifting him off his feet. He settles down next to Rundi.

"We wanted to see our friends before we leave here and head north," Rundi tells them. "I don't think we'll be back. If anyone would like to come along, we'd be glad to have you."

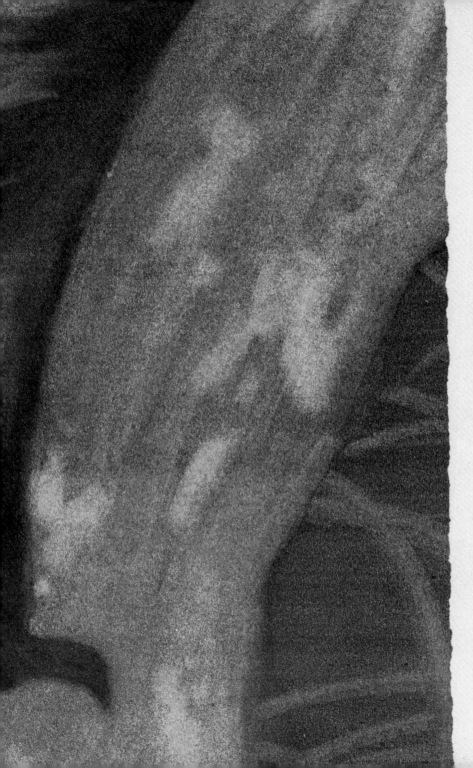

"I don't want you to go," says Big Brown Bat. "Why are you leaving us?"

Coati wiggles his nose and says, "I want to travel away from dangerous hunt-dogs."

"I want to find a place with more forest wild and fewer fences," answers Rundi.

"There will always be danger," says Big Brown Bat. "Do as I do—adapt to the changes. Bats can live in barns, in churches, and almost anywhere. If you try, so can you."

"I do try," says Coati, "but I must always watch my back. Even puppies practice chasing me. Settlers want to catch me and eat me!"

The animals shudder. They growl low, muttering.

Then Rundi says, "I feel unsafe to be out in the open, in the cleared land. And there are no more jaguarundis here."

Says the orange-yellow ocelot, "My friend, I, too, am alone. And everywhere I go, there are walls to stop me, traps and hunters to catch me. Some day, I'll have to leave, too. Then I'll go south over the mountains."

As the moon slides across the night, the animals talk on. Much later, Rundi sums up: "Some of us are many, and others of us are few. But we're all afraid of what might come."

Ringtail squeaks, "In the future, I think there'll be more farms, less canopy, and fewer of us."

"Change your ways, or else!" warns Big Brown Bat. "Adapt is what we must do."

The powerful jaguar with the golden, spotted coat speaks up: "Day in, year out, hunters keep up their war. They want to sell my hide. But they will never destroy *me*!"

Some animals cringe in fear. Others bare their teeth.

"Each time I catch their scent," says Jaguar, "I turn about and race away. Oh, no!" he gloats. "I'll never flee, nor change my ways. I'll stay in these parts, hiding when I have to."

"That's the way to do it!" Kit Fox says. "That's it! Rundi, I've made up my mind. I will stay here and take my chances."

"Unwise! Unwise!" chatters Coati. "Run. Run with us!"

"No, you stay, too, Coati and Rundi! Stay with us," cry others.

The night is nearly over. The animals have spoken together. Each thinks and wonders how much time it has to be safe here.

"We plan to keep moving until we reach the north,"
Rundi tells them.

"If you must go, then good luck, Rundi! Take care, Coati!"
Animals call softly up and down the field, "Good-bye,
good friends, good-bye!"

"Good-bye, friends, and good night!" Rundi and Coati
answer.

The moon goes down. The animals leave. Finally the
Great Pineapple Field is silent. The fallen timber log seems
more lifeless than ever, slowly sinking into the ground.
Before sunrise, Rundi and Coati begin their journey to
the Rio Bravo.

Days later, they reach the river. "Oh, no!" cries Rundi. They find desert heat and more scrubland, houses and settlers, cats and dogs, cotton patches and cornfields. In the distance are cities, one on each side of the river. And everywhere, fences.

Rundi and Coati look on in silence. Finally, Rundi says, "Let's cross the waters, see if it's better over there."

"I'm too tired to travel anymore," old Coati answers. But he clings to Rundi's tail as the agile cat swims the way across. There, the Rio Bravo is called the Rio Grande. They squeeze beneath a high fence.

At once, a pack of dogs catches their scent. Rundi and Coati outrun them. Wet and shivering, they hide for hours in the shadowy corner of a lean-to. Finally, the dogs give up.

"Nothing much changes," whines Coati.

"Big Brown Bat said it. It is we who must change."

Coati follows Rundi. They find a prickly pear bush, and Coati stops to eat a piece. "Ummm, good!" he chatters.

"I'll go on ahead," calls Rundi.

With his mouth full of juicy pear, Coati calls softly back—"Be careful!"

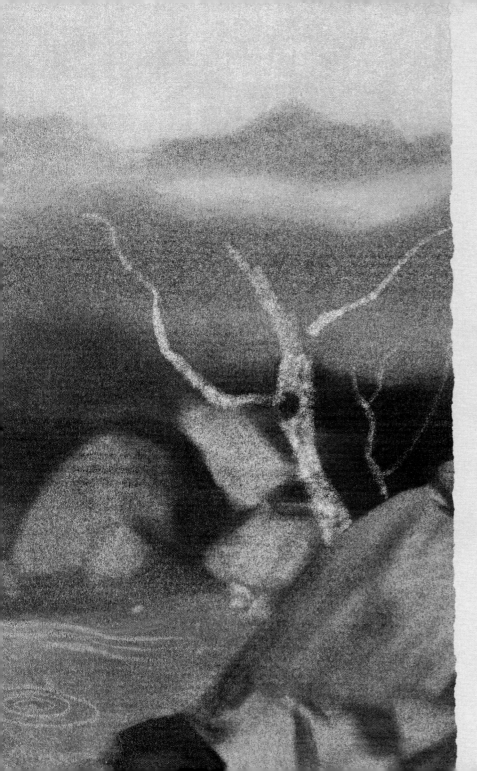

The search for a home drives Rundi on. At evening, he is surprised to come upon a red jaguarundi on the move.

"So glad to meet you!" he greets the female cat.

"And you! Hello!" says she. Together, they prowl along the night. Each is happy to have the other's company.

A pretty pair, Rundi and Red Rundi Cat together go hunting for a habitat.

"Look! There are thickets!" Rundi exclaims. They thread their way within the tangled reach of brush and thorny mesquite.

"How cool the shade is all around," says Red Rundi Cat.

"Ah, yes," purrs Rundi, stretching out. "Oh, I'm tired! Let's stay here now and make our den." Red Rundi Cat agrees, and they settle in.

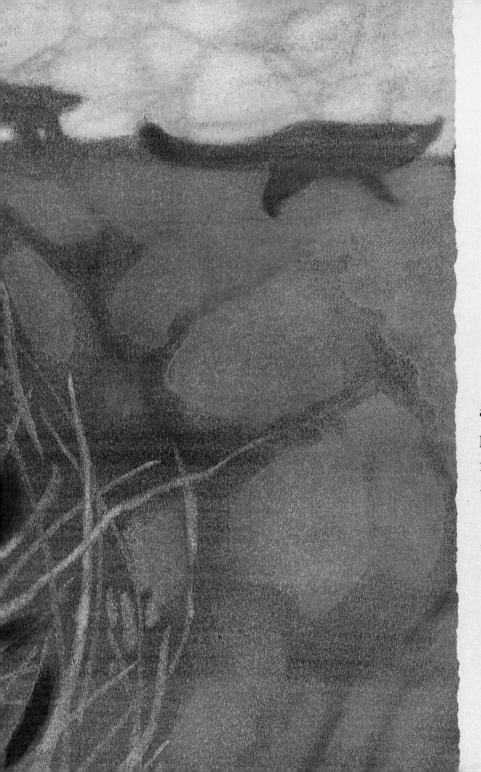

Not far away, Coati comes upon shrubs and stunted acacia trees. He finds lizards and scorpions and more prickly pear bushes. He roots for tubers and grubs. He naps. It is his old habit to stay by himself. He knows he will see Rundi on the trails.

One blistering day, he spies a band of coatimundis on the move. "I can't keep up with you," he murmurs. "But I'm glad to see you are close by."

When Coati is ready to sleep for the night, he climbs a tree. He dreams he's running with his family band. Coati Coatimundi is content.

Long, dry days and pleasant, cool nights go by. In Rundi's den, a litter of three spotted kittens is born. The kittens eat and play. "See how they grow!" says Rundi. "One turns dark; one, gray; and one, red."

"They'll soon be on their own," Red Rundi says. "But will they be safe?"

"Let's hope so," Rundi answers. He gazes wistfully at the kittens playing. "The north must be farther on," Rundi adds. "I know we'll find it. We must!"

"Oh, I'm sure of it," says Red Rundi Cat. "There are land dwellers who take care to protect their forests. They plant saplings. I have seen them."

"Then someday, we'll go north, and there we'll find our crown canopy at last," Rundi tells her. "But for now..."

"For now...?" Red Rundi asks.

"For now, we stay put," says Rundi. "As Big Brown Bat said, we adapt."

"We know how to take care of ourselves," Red Rundi says.

Rundi Jaguarundi and Red Rundi fit into their habitat. They teach the kittens how to stalk and prowl, how to find food.

They *live*.

THE END

# ABOUT THE ANIMALS IN THIS BOOK

WHILE SOME of the animals in this book are endangered, others are shy and so rarely seen that we do not know how many exist. We do know that our destruction of their habitat makes their struggle for survival more and more difficult.

The **jaguarundi** (pronounced ja'gwa run'dē) is a small, solitary wild cat from the Central and South American rain forests. It has a sleek coat, a long body, and short legs. Jaguarundis are dichromatic — having two or three color varieties. Red, gray, or black kittens are often born in the same litter. These color variations help jaguarundis blend into the brush and grass landscape. The cats often live near water on the edges of forests, and they are excellent runners. Their prey are mainly rodents and ground birds. Jaguarundis are shy, secretive cats, now found in Arizona and Texas. Rarely seen, they may well be endangered.

The **coati** (pronounced kwa ti) is a member of the raccoon family that lives in the forests of Central and South America. Coatis look like raccoons with bushy tails, but they also have long, flexible snouts, and their coats can be shades of red, brown, yellow, or black. A middle-aged male coati is called a coatimundi, and the term is often used for all coatis. Older males are usually solitary. But coatis are social animals that travel in troops. They eat anything, from small animals and insects to fruits and seeds. Immensely curious, they are very adaptable.

The **kit fox** is found in deserts from the southwestern United States down to northern Mexico. Kit foxes have such large ears that they are also known as big-eared foxes. They are trusting, nocturnal animals that live in burrows and eat rabbits, insects, mice, and rats. Kit foxes are threatened with extinction from predators and humans.

The **owl monkey** is also called the night monkey, and it lives in the South American forests. It is the only nocturnal monkey in the New World (the Americas). At sundown the monkeys start moving around, searching for fruit, leaves, insects, small birds, and mammals. Owl monkeys have huge eyes, which help them see at night, when they are most active. They live in small family groups, sleeping in trees high above the ground. Owl monkeys are now rare animals.

The **bush dog**'s varied habitat stretches from Panama to much of northeastern South America. Bush dogs look like small bears, or badgers, with their stocky bodies and short legs. Shy and seldom seen, they are nocturnal animals found in forests and grasslands. They live and hunt in packs, are good swimmers, and they eat small animals. Bush dogs are rare.

The **maned wolf** is found in marshlands and grassy areas from Brazil to Argentina. Despite its name, the maned wolf is a member of the dog family (Canidae). It looks like a long-legged fox with pointed ears held straight up, and has a reddish-brown mane of thick fur along its back. It is an elusive animal, living in remote areas alone or in pairs. It hunts by lying in wait, then ambushing small creatures, which it immediately swallows. Farmers believe it eats livestock. The maned wolf has been virtually wiped out.

The **capuchin monkey** (pronounced kap' yōō chin) is also known as the ringtail monkey. Capuchin monkeys are usually black or dark brown with white faces, and they live in groups among the treetops of Central and South America. They descend to the ground only to drink. They eat mostly fruit, and swing and jump from tree to tree.

The **ringtail cat** has a striped tail longer than its body. Ringtail cats are yellowish-gray in color, with catlike bodies and foxlike faces. They live in forests and rocky terrain from Oregon to Mexico. Sharp claws allow them to climb walls or trees. The bobcat, great horned owl, and humans are its chief predators. Ringtail cats adapt well to gardens and city parks.

The **tayra** (pronounced tī ra), of the weasel family, has a long neck supporting a head that is quite large in relation to its slender body. Tayras range from southern Mexico to Argentina. They live in forests, woodlands, and other areas rich in vegetation. They are solitary, but hunt in groups for guinea pigs, squirrels, and, often, poultry. They particularly like sweet fruits.

The **kinkajou** (pronounced king' ka jōō), a member of the raccoon family and related to the coatimundi, has soft, brownish fur and rounded ears. Kinkajous are agile as acrobats, hanging by their long, grasping tails from tree limbs. Rarely leaving the trees, they inhabit forests from Mexico to Brazil. They are commonly kept as pets and treated gently. But when frightened or angry, they are known to bite sharply.

The **big brown bat** is a widespread North American species found from southern Canada to Colombia and Venezuela, and to the West Indies. They are medium-sized bats with dark, broad muzzles, simple noses, and long, brown fur. Originally forest dwellers, they now inhabit nearly all situations from caves to urban buildings and under bridges. Big brown bats are somewhat slow, heavy flyers that sleep all day and fly out at night to hunt insects. They live in large groups and are known to keep themselves very clean. They hibernate in winter.

The **ocelot** (pronounced os' lot) is an American wildcat living in forests or brush-covered regions from Texas to much of South America. Ocelots hunt reptiles, birds, and medium-sized mammals, chiefly at night. Largely solitary animals, they rest in trees, often hunting in them. They live in pairs. Their beautifully patterned coats are greatly sought after commercially. The result has been that the species has disappeared over a great part of its range. The ocelot is considered endangered.

The **jaguar** (pronounced jag' war) has a yellow-and-black-spotted coat and is the largest wildcat of the Americas. Jaguars are powerfully built, are approximately 6–9 feet in length, including tails of 2–3 feet, and can weigh as much as 350 pounds. Often, they live near water on the edge of canopied forests. They are good climbers and swimmers; they eat large and small animals, from rodents and fish to alligators and cattle. Jaguars are hunted relentlessly for their sleek, orange-tan fur with black spots arranged in rosettes. A solitary predator, the jaguar is seriously endangered.

The **spotted cavy**, or paca, lives in the forests of Central and South America. It is a rodent that has features resembling those of the guinea pig. Spotted cavies have huge eyes and feed at night on fruit, leaves, and bark. Their dark brownish coats with white markings and stripes on the back help them hide in the brush. Nocturnal, they sleep in burrows during the day. Spotted cavies are hunted for their fat and tasty flesh.

The **bobcat** lives in mountains, deserts, forests, and grasslands from southern Canada to Mexico. Its soft coat varies in color but is usually brown with black markings. A solitary animal, it lives in well-marked territories and burrows or dens in places where it rests. It is known to migrate. Bobcats prey upon small animals, especially rabbits, and are resourceful in their search for food. They are hunted and trapped by humans for their thick fur.

The **white-tailed deer** is a common woodland deer ranging from southern Canada to South America. Its summer coat is reddish-brown. In winter, it wears gray-brown. Only males have antlers. Its habitat is temperate to tropical deciduous forest. White-tailed deer gather in small herds and are not endangered.

The **howler monkey** is the largest South American monkey, and it lives in the rain forests from southern Mexico to Argentina. Howlers are noted for their deep hooting, and roaring calls, which carry two or three miles. They live in groups and have black, brown, or red fur; they eat leaves, bugs, flowers, fruit, and nuts. Some species of howler monkey are endangered.

## ABOUT THE AUTHOR

VIRGINIA HAMILTON is one of the most distinguished writers in America. She has been awarded the Newbery Medal, the international Hans Christian Andersen Medal, the Laura Ingalls Wilder Medal, the National Book Award, the Coretta Scott King Award, the Regina Medal, the *Boston Globe-Horn Book* Award, and three honorary doctorates, including one from the Bank Street College of Education. In addition, she is the only children's book author to have been awarded a MacArthur Fellowship. Her novel *M.C. Higgins the Great* was awarded the Newbery Medal and the *Boston Globe-Horn Book* Award, and three of her books, *Sweet Whispers, Brother Rush; The Planet of Junior Brown;* and the folklore collection, *In the Beginning: Creation Stories from Around the World* are Newbery Honor Books. Her other books of folklore include *Her Stories: African American Folktales, Fairy Tales, and True Tales* and *The People Could Fly*, both Coretta Scott King Award winners; and *Many Thousand Gone: African Americans from Slavery to Freedom.* Her 1993 novel *Plain City* was an ALA Notable Book, and her 1996 collection *When Birds Could Talk & Bats Could Sing* received five starred reviews. Virginia Hamilton lives in Ohio with her husband, poet Arnold Adoff.

## ABOUT THE ILLUSTRATOR

FLOYD COOPER was born and raised in Tulsa, Oklahoma. Among the books he has illustrated are *Grandpa's Face*, by Eloise Greenfield, an ALA Notable Book and a *School Library Journal* Best Book of the Year; *Pass It On: African-American Poetry for Children*, a 1993 *American Bookseller* Pick of the Lists; and *Brown Honey in Broomwheat Tea*, a 1994 Coretta Scott King Honor Book for Illustration.